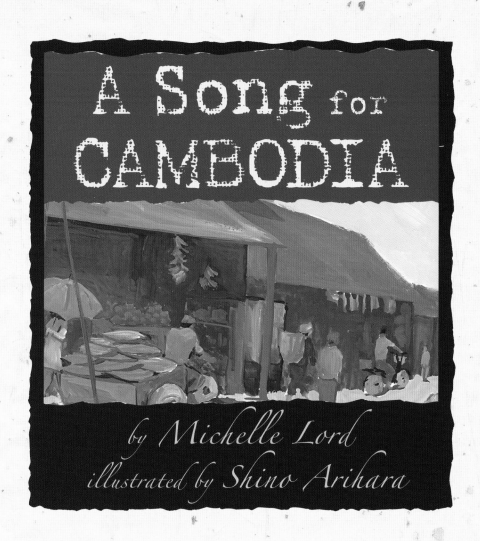

A Song for CAMBODIA

by Michelle Lord

illustrated by Shino Arihara

Lee & Low Books Inc.
New York

For my wonderful mother . . . I don't want to imagine
never hearing your sweet voice—*M.L.*

For Tang—*S.A.*

ACKNOWLEDGMENT
A special thanks to Arn for sharing your story with me. I hope I've done
your memories justice. You are an inspiration—turning your horrific tragedy
into healing—helping lost songs find new ears.—M.L.

Text copyright © 2008 by Michelle Lord
Illustrations copyright © 2008 by Shino Arihara

LEE & LOW BOOKS Inc., 95 Madison Avenue, New York, NY 10016
leeandlow.com

Manufactured in China

Book design by Christy Hale
Book production by The Kids at Our House

The text is set in Berkeley Book
The illustrations are rendered in gouache

10 9 8 7 6 5 4 3 2 1
First Edition

Library of Congress Cataloging-in-Publication Data
Lord, Michelle.
A song for Cambodia / by Michelle Lord ; illustrated by Shino Arihara. — 1st ed.
p. cm.
Summary: "A biography of Arn Chorn-Pond who, as a young boy in 1970s Cambodia, survived
the Khmer Rouge killing fields because of his skill on the khim, a traditional instrument, and
later went on to help heal others and revive Cambodian music and culture"—Provided by publisher.
ISBN 978-1-60060-139-2
1. Chorn-Pond, Arn—Juvenile literature. 2. Musicians—Cambodia—
Biography—Juvenile literature. I. Arihara, Shino, ill. II. Title.
ML3920.C465L67 2008
959.604'2092—dc22
[B]   2007026248

foreword

In 1975 the Khmer Rouge, rebel soldiers, took hold of the Cambodian capital, Phnom Penh. Led by Pol Pot, the soldiers wanted to make the Kingdom of Cambodia a communist country. Everything would belong to the government, and all citizens would benefit equally. This plan, however, went terribly wrong. Using violence and terror, the Khmer Rouge made their way through village after village. The soldiers killed or captured civilians and members of the old government. Families were torn apart. Markets and money, art and books, temples and monasteries, schools and businesses were all destroyed.

As part of the plan, the Khmer Rouge wanted Cambodia to be self-sufficient and not rely on other countries for food. The soldiers set up work camps throughout the country to grow rice. Camp borders were surrounded with land mines and guards so no one could escape. All Cambodians—young and old, sick or starving—were forced into the hard labor of growing rice. They cleared land, built dikes, dug canals, planted seedlings, and harvested grain. Businessmen, scholars, and artists labored in the fields while former peasants watched over them. Children did not attend school but were trained to work and spy on their elders. Anyone who did not obey was beaten or killed.

The Khmer Rouge ruled Cambodia until 1979, when the Vietnamese invaded and removed them from power. During Pol Pot's reign approximately 1.7 million Cambodian men, women, and children lost their lives. Those who survived did so any way that they could.

In a country of sugar palms, whispering grasses, and bright sunshine there lived a boy named Arn. His home was filled with the sweet sounds of music and laughter. He danced with his eleven brothers and sisters while his grandparents sang songs of long ago. His mother hummed to the little ones while she worked. His father taught the older children operas in the evenings.

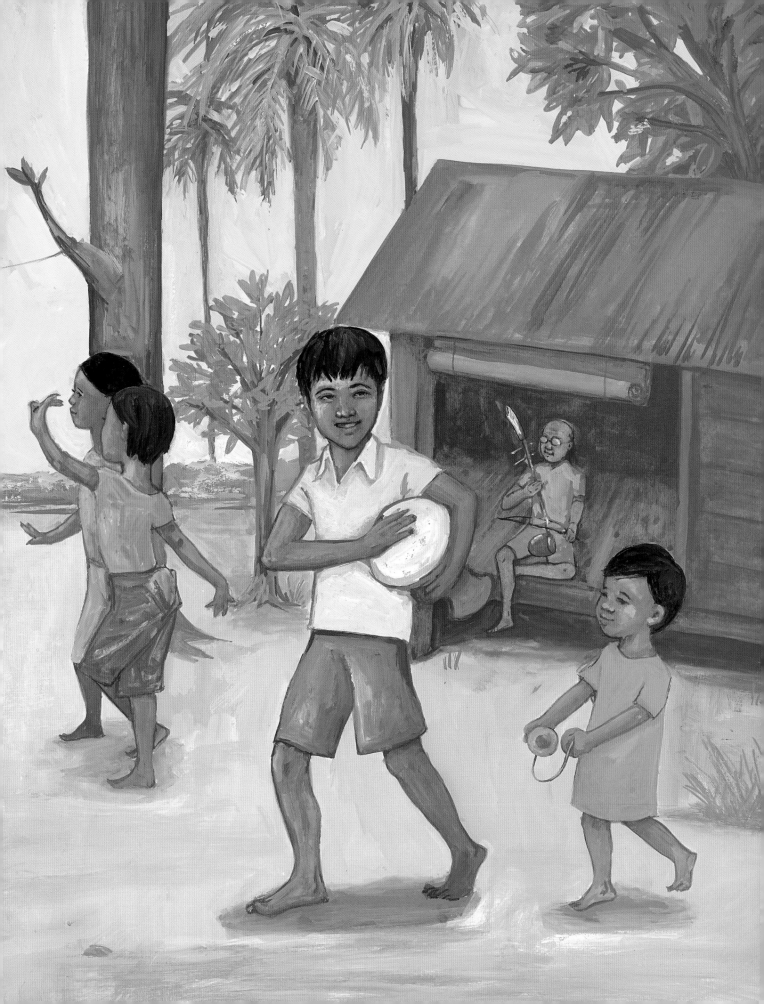

In Arn's village in northern Cambodia, fresh fruits and vegetables filled the open-air markets. Arn and other boys of eight and nine plucked silvery fish by the dozen from flowing rivers. Water buffalo grazed in the countryside. Long-legged cranes danced on the shore, and flower gardens grew alongside homes.

Arn's family took offerings of food to the orange-robed Buddhist monks. Sounds of gongs mixed with the songs of birds and the laughter of children.

During the hottest months of 1975 the sun dimmed in the smoky sky. Explosions crackled through the air like a thousand New Year's noisemakers. The ground shook. A group of soldiers called the Khmer Rouge, or "Red Khmers," spread through the land like army ants, stripping everything in their path. Hospitals were emptied and temples crushed. Schools were made into prisons and books burned in fires. Songbirds stopped chirping, and monks were silenced. Art, religion, and music disappeared from people's lives.

Some areas near Cambodia were used to the sounds of war. While Cambodia remained neutral, the war between the United States and Cambodia's neighbor Vietnam had often spilled across the border. Arn lived far from this fighting, far from the American planes that bombed the countryside—so when Arn and his family heard unfamiliar explosions, they were afraid.

Steadily the sounds of fighting grew closer, until the day came when the Khmer Rouge reached Arn's village. Soldiers with hard faces pointed rifles. They ordered families out of their homes and herded them into groups.

When the soldiers arrived at Arn's home, his heart beat faster and

louder than any drum. The soldiers separated Arn and his family to go to different work camps. There was nothing they could do. In the last moments, they shouted tearful goodbyes. Arn clutched his mother, but soldiers forced them apart. She cried out for her children, then was gone. Arn would never hear her voice again.

After a long hard journey Arn stumbled into a children's work camp, empty-handed and brokenhearted. Around him, Arn saw children of all ages. They were each given sets of dark clothes, but no shoes.

Arn worked in the rice paddies from sunrise to midnight. He

labored under the blazing sun and in monsoon rains. His bare feet
blistered and his belly bulged, even though it was always empty. Rice
had become more prized than gemstones, which meant little of it was
wasted on the young workers. If they were lucky, the children caught
dragonflies, beetles, or grubs to eat.

Sweet sounds no longer filled Arn's world. He and the other
children worked for hours in silence because talking was forbidden.
All that broke the quiet were the shouts of soldiers threatening young
workers and the rumbles of Arn's empty belly. Arn yearned for his
home, full of joyful music and the comfort of his mother's hum.

The silence became deafening. In time it seemed as if even the soldiers could not live without music. One day they asked for volunteers to join a musical group. The group would play revolutionary and marching songs. Bravely Arn raised a shaky hand. He and five others were chosen to learn to play the *khim*, a wooden string instrument.

Arn's father had told his son that Cambodian music existed only in memory. Songs were passed down from a parent to a child or from a master to a student. There were no written compositions.

A man with white hair and sad eyes became Arn's teacher. The master taught his students to play different notes by striking strings on the khim with bamboo mallets. Soon a stream of notes blended into a song. Arn knew he must play his best for his life depended on pleasing the soldiers. In only five days Arn became the best student.

Soon after Arn and the others learned to play, a soldier gathered the teacher and all but the two best khim players. The group marched to the sweet-smelling orange groves, and the soldier returned alone.

Arn mourned the death of the teacher whose name he never knew, but he held his pain deep inside. Arn could be killed if he was caught crying.

The gentle sound of the khim was heaven to Arn. When
he practiced he thought of a world far from the pain and
suffering of the work camp. Songs filled Arn's empty stomach
and soothed his broken heart. Hidden feelings flowed through
him as the mallets struck various tones on the khim.

Arn tapped out his songs while the other children worked. He saw them tilt their heads to catch the tunes in the muggy air. A few closed their eyes as they twisted rice seedlings into the muddy ground. The music took them far from the rice fields too.

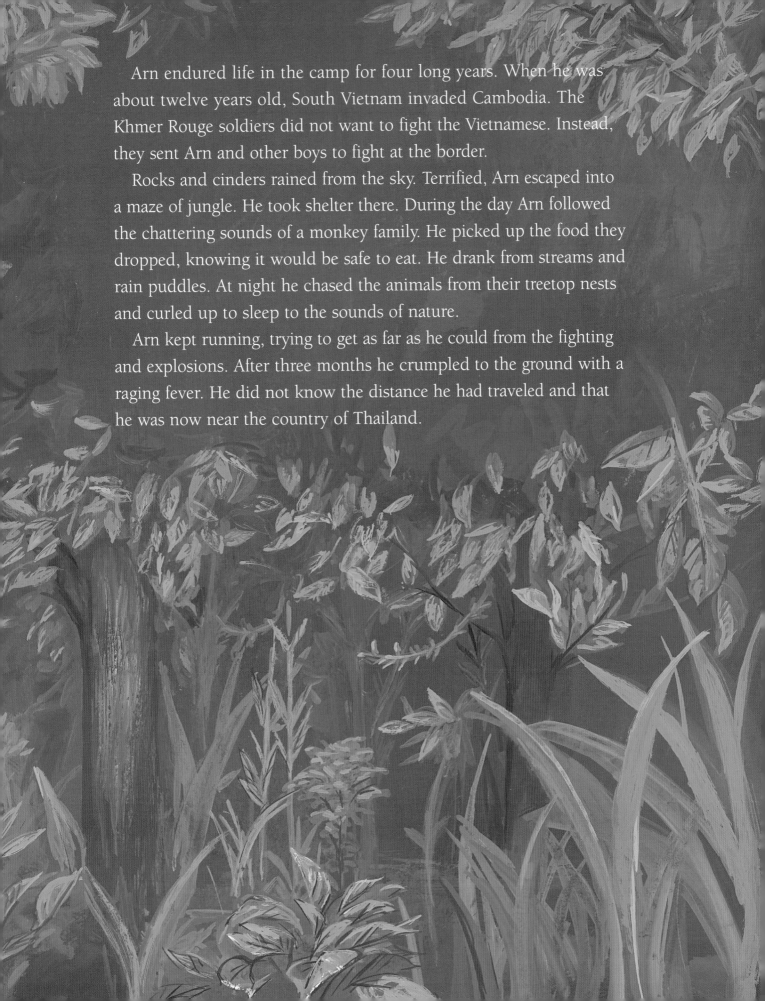

Arn endured life in the camp for four long years. When he was about twelve years old, South Vietnam invaded Cambodia. The Khmer Rouge soldiers did not want to fight the Vietnamese. Instead, they sent Arn and other boys to fight at the border.

Rocks and cinders rained from the sky. Terrified, Arn escaped into a maze of jungle. He took shelter there. During the day Arn followed the chattering sounds of a monkey family. He picked up the food they dropped, knowing it would be safe to eat. He drank from streams and rain puddles. At night he chased the animals from their treetop nests and curled up to sleep to the sounds of nature.

Arn kept running, trying to get as far as he could from the fighting and explosions. After three months he crumpled to the ground with a raging fever. He did not know the distance he had traveled and that he was now near the country of Thailand.

Arn awoke in the Sakeo Refugee Camp. Two girls had found him at the border of Cambodia and Thailand and helped bring him to the camp. Workers there nursed Arn until his fever broke.

In the refugee camp Arn was free from the Khmer Rouge soldiers and the fighting, but life was very hard there too. Food was scarce, days were long, and the aid workers left each night. The orphans in the camp feared they would be sold back to the Khmer Rouge by the Thai soldiers who guarded the camp after dark. Afraid and lonely, Arn longed for the comforting music of his khim.

    One day a flood swept through the camp. Arn was too weak to help himself. He would have drowned if a tall man had not plucked him from the murky floodwaters.

    Arn became friends with the American volunteer who had saved him, Reverend Peter Pond. Arn and Reverend Peter did not speak each other's languages. They communicated with hand signals and smiles. Day by day their relationship grew stronger, and Arn began to feel less lonely. Before returning to the United States, Reverend Peter decided to adopt Arn.

Arn arrived in the United States when he was fourteen years old. Stepping off the plane, Arn ran and tried to hide. The bright lights of the airport reminded him of flashing gunfire without the sound.

There were many things for Arn to get used to in his new country. He slept on a mattress and went to school in a large

building for the first time. Ketchup became his favorite food.

Arn was safe and had enough to eat. His body grew stronger, but inside, his heart still ached with the loss of his family in Cambodia. He had nightmares, and they frightened him. Since Arn did not speak much English, he couldn't express how he felt.

Arn asked Reverend Peter to find him a khim and a Cambodian flute, a *khloy*. Soon, single notes became melodies and Arn made music again. In time he began to play for other people and learned to talk to them about his life in Cambodia. Through playing his music and telling his story, Arn slowly began to heal on the inside too.

Over the years Arn's nightmares transformed into a dream—a dream of helping his homeland. With his heart once again full of sweet sounds, Arn vowed to return to his country of sugar palms, whispering grasses, and bright sunshine to help others with his music.

afterword

In 1984 Arn Chorn-Pond founded the Children of War Organization to teach teenagers in the United States about the horrors of war and hate. Arn then returned to Cambodia during the summers of 1986, 1987, and 1988. "I must go back," he said, "and try to help rebuild Cambodia, but also rebuild my own life."

Almost ten years after the end of the Khmer Rouge and Pol Pot's rule, Cambodia was still in shambles. The lush green countryside was riddled with millions of land mines. The people struggled to rebuild their lives, their families, and the centuries of culture that had been destroyed. Arn helped fellow survivors in refugee camps, explaining, "the more good things that I do to help and care for others' suffering—not just my own—I know that I will find myself free from my own suffering and from my own horrible past."

Arn received the Reebok Human Rights Award in 1988 for his work with survivors of war. In 1991 he founded Cambodian Volunteers for Community Development to encourage community service and cultural rebuilding in Cambodia. In the United States, Arn worked with gang members and other at-risk youth. He showed teens how to express their feelings through music, not violence. Arn was awarded the Spirit of Anne Frank Award in 1996 for his humanitarian work.

Despite these accomplishments, Arn still felt a void in his life. "I come from a family of performers," he said. "I am the only one left." In 1998 Arn created the Cambodian Living Arts program to revive the traditional art forms of Cambodia and also to inspire contemporary artistic expression. Returning again to Cambodia, Arn searched high and low for the musical masters of long ago. He found an old opera star digging through trash. A percussionist trained at the Royal Palace was wandering the streets homeless. A master of wind instruments who was left partially deaf by gunfire was living in a crumbling shack. Other once-famous artists were working as taxi drivers or barbers. Arn brought them together to record their songs and to teach children traditional Cambodian music.

Today Arn Chorn-Pond continues his efforts to revive Cambodian classical arts, music, and instrument crafting. When Arn was a young boy, music saved his life. Now it is Arn's mission to save the music.

Everyone has good and bad within them. It's up to us to decide how to live. You can literally change the world.
—Arn Chorn-Pond

Arn Chorn-Pond in front of the house he is building in Cambodia.